On the First Day

of First Grade

For my grandson, Cole, with love—T.R.
For my brother, Jack x—S.J.

On the First Day

# of First Grade

by Tish Rabe pictures by Sarah Jennings

HARPER
An Imprint of HarperCollinsPublishers

On the first day of first grade
I had fun right away

laughing and learning all day!

On the second day of first grade

I had fun right away

helping in my classroom

and laughing and learning all day!

On the third day of first grade

I had fun right away

choosing books to read,

helping in my classroom,

and laughing and learning all day!

On the fourth day of first grade

I had fun right away

planting little seeds,

choosing books to read,

helping in my classroom,

and laughing and learning all day!

On the fifth day of first grade

I had fun right away

TELLING THE TIME!

planting little seeds,

choosing books to read,

helping in my classroom,

and laughing and learning all day!

On the sixth day of first grade

I had fun right away

leading friends in line,

TELLING THE TIME!

planting little seeds,

choosing books to read,

helping in my classroom,

and laughing and learning all day!

On the seventh day of first grade

I had fun right away

building things with clay,

leading friends in line,

TELLING THE TIME!

planting little seeds,

choosing books to read,

helping in my classroom,

and laughing and learning all day!

On the eighth day of first grade

I had fun right away

performing in a play,

building things with clay,

leading friends in line,

TELLING THE TIME!

planting little seeds,

choosing books to read,

helping in my classroom,

and laughing and learning all day!

On the ninth day of first grade

I had fun right away

throwing a ball,

performing in a play,

building things with clay,

leading friends in line,

TELLING THE TIME!

planting little seeds,

choosing books to read,

helping in my classroom,

and laughing and learning all day!

On the tenth day of first grade
I had fun right away

playing a song,

throwing a ball,

performing in a play,

building things with clay,

leading friends in line,

TELLING THE TIME!
planting little seeds,
choosing books to read,
helping in my classroom,
and laughing and learning all day!

On the eleventh day of first grade

I had fun right away

counting with coins,

playing a song,

throwing a ball,

performing in a play,

building things with clay,

leading friends in line,

TELLING THE TIME!

planting little seeds,

choosing books to read,

helping in my classroom,

and laughing and learning all day!

On the twelfth day of first grade

I had fun right away

showing my pet bunny,

counting with coins,

playing a song,

throwing a ball,

performing in a play,

building things with clay,

leading friends in line,

TELLING THE TIME!

planting little seeds,

choosing books to read,

helping in my classroom,

and laughing and learning all day!

FIRST GRADE IS So FUN!